Pinocchio

Anna Bowles

Richard Watson

LITTLE TIGER

LONDON

One day, Geppetto the old carpenter
decided to make a puppet. He worked
very skilfully and when the puppet was
finished it looked like it was alive.
Its mouth opened . . . and it
blew a raspberry. "THFFFFT!"
Pinocchio *was* alive!

Pinocchio cried, "You look **boring**. I want to see the world!" The naughty puppet ran outside – SMACK! into a pair of legs.

"What's all this?" grumbled the policeman. "Is that man chasing you?"

"Yes! He's a robber," Pinocchio lied.

Then a very strange thing happened. Pinocchio's nose began to grow longer . . .

Meanwhile, Geppetto was dragged off to jail!

Pinocchio sat at home feeling very pleased with himself. Suddenly, he heard a little voice . . .

Crik, crik!

"I am the Talking Cricket!" it said. "I will give you some advice to help you become a real boy.

Be good and kind and always do what adults tell you . . ."

"Boring!"

Pinocchio cried, chasing the cricket away.

But it would be nice to be a real boy . . .

Kind old Geppetto forgave Pinocchio for sending him to jail.

"How do I become a real boy?" Pinocchio asked.

"You will need to go to school," said Geppetto kindly.

"Oh," Pinocchio sighed.
That sounded no fun at all.

Boring!

"I'll go!" Pinocchio promised. But as he
spoke his nose grew longer and **longer** . . .

Geppetto sold his coat so he could buy Pinocchio a schoolbook. Pinocchio was so grateful he decided to go to school after all.

But on the way he saw a sign . . .

Pinocchio sold his book and bought a ticket.
"I've come to play!" he announced to the puppets.

They high-fived and
danced all day.

It was dark when Pinocchio left the theatre.

"Be careful!" warned the other puppets. But Pinocchio thought he was so clever he had nothing to be scared of.

Pinocchio was stopped by two horrible thieves.

Hello...

...little puppet.

"Don't hurt me. I haven't got any money!" Pinocchio said.

At last Pinocchio escaped. He ran until he reached a little house.

A kind fairy lived in the house.
She put Pinocchio to bed
where he tossed and turned.
"I'm ill!" he groaned.

The fairy brought
him medicine.

"That looks horrible!
I won't drink it!"

"Will!"

"Won't!"

"Will!"

"What if I don't?"

"You'll die."

Sometimes it is a good
idea to do what adults say.

Sometimes . . .

When Pinocchio was better
he left the fairy's house.
He wanted to find something fun
to do, but instead he kept
thinking about home.

"I wonder what my father
is doing?" he said.
A pigeon heard him and landed on the road.

"I've seen your father searching for you. He's terribly worried!"

"I don't care!" Pinocchio snapped.

But to his amazement, his nose grew longer . . .

and longer . . . and longer!

He *did* care about Geppetto. Very much.

"I saw Geppetto rowing across the sea to look for you," said the pigeon.

"Can you tell him I'm here?" asked Pinocchio.

"Tell him yourself," the pigeon retorted, scooping Pinocchio onto his back and flying off.

"WaaaaAAAAARGH!"

When he'd got over his fright, Pinocchio peered down at the sea below. He saw . . .

a floating oar . . .

Geppetto's empty boat . . .

and a

HUGE SHARK!

"FATHER!" cried Pinocchio.

He wriggled so much that he fell off the pigeon.

Pinocchio tumbled **plop** into the ocean.

First he sank

down . . . .

Then rocketed **up** . . . .

Geppetto!

Pinocchio and his father hugged each other.

"I'm afraid we're trapped," said Geppetto. "Even if we escape from the shark, I'll drown."

Pinocchio laughed.

"I'm made of wood! I can float you to shore."

They crept up the
shark's throat.
Pinocchio reached out
to tickle its nose . . .

ATISSHHHOOOO!!

They were free!

When they made it to the shore,
Pinocchio was too tired to walk.
Geppetto carried him home,
and they slept beside each other
all night.

When he woke up, Pinocchio cried,
"Father, are you all right?"
"Yes, my son," said Geppetto. "And look
what has happened to you."
While Pinocchio was asleep, he had
transformed. Smiling in the mirror he
saw a good, kind, amazing . . .

REAL boy!